Dinosaurs

SIZES
Compared with man

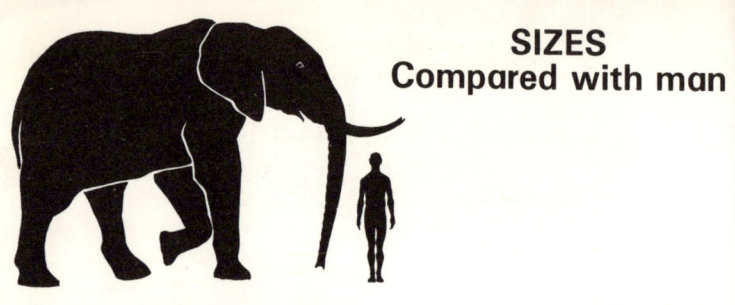

Present-day Elephant

Mammoth

Stegosaurus

Pteranodon

Baluchitherium

Diplodocus

Tyrannosaurus

LADYBIRD BOOKS, INC.
Lewiston, Maine 04240 U.S.A.
© LADYBIRD BOOKS LTD MCMLXXIV
Loughborough, Leicestershire, England

All rights reserved. No part of this publication may be reproduced, stored in a retrieval system, or transmitted in any form or by any means, electronic, mechanical, photocopying, recording or otherwise, without the prior consent of the copyright owner.

Printed in England

Dinosaurs

Written by Colin Douglas
Illustrated by B. H. Robinson

Ladybird Books

In the beginning, the world must have

At first, nothing lived on the land or in the sea.

oked like this:

There were no plants, no animals, and no people.

Life began in the sea.

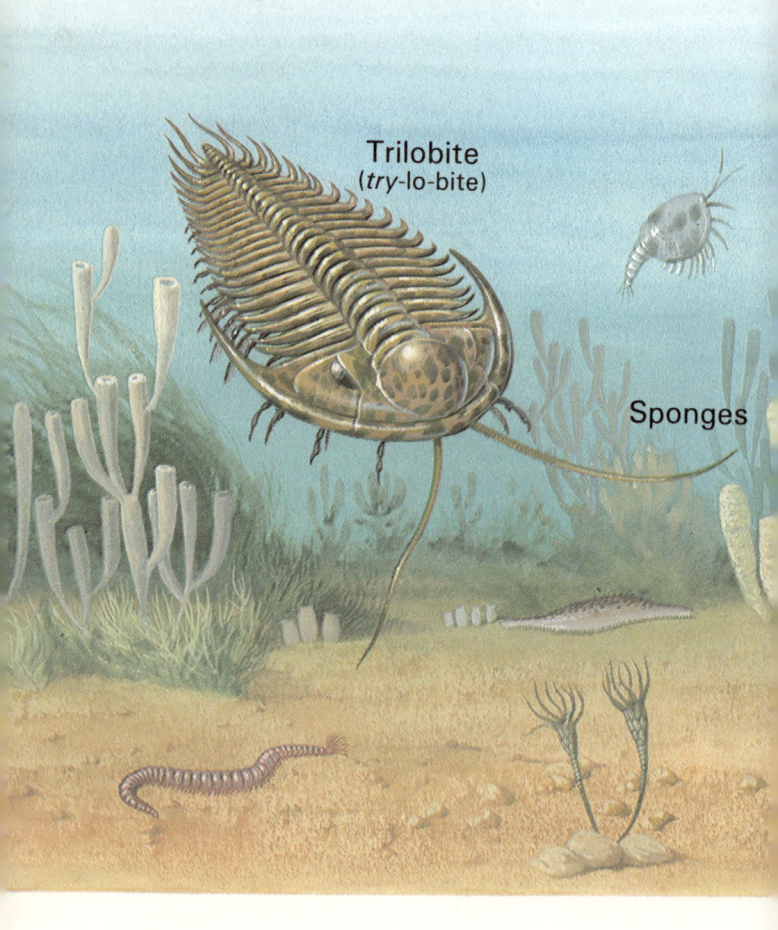

Trilobite
(*try*-lo-bite)

Sponges

Life began in the sea.
The first living things
were very, very small.
Some grew into tiny worms.

Later, there were jellyfish, starfish, and sponges.

Later still, there were living things that had shells.

The Age of Fishes

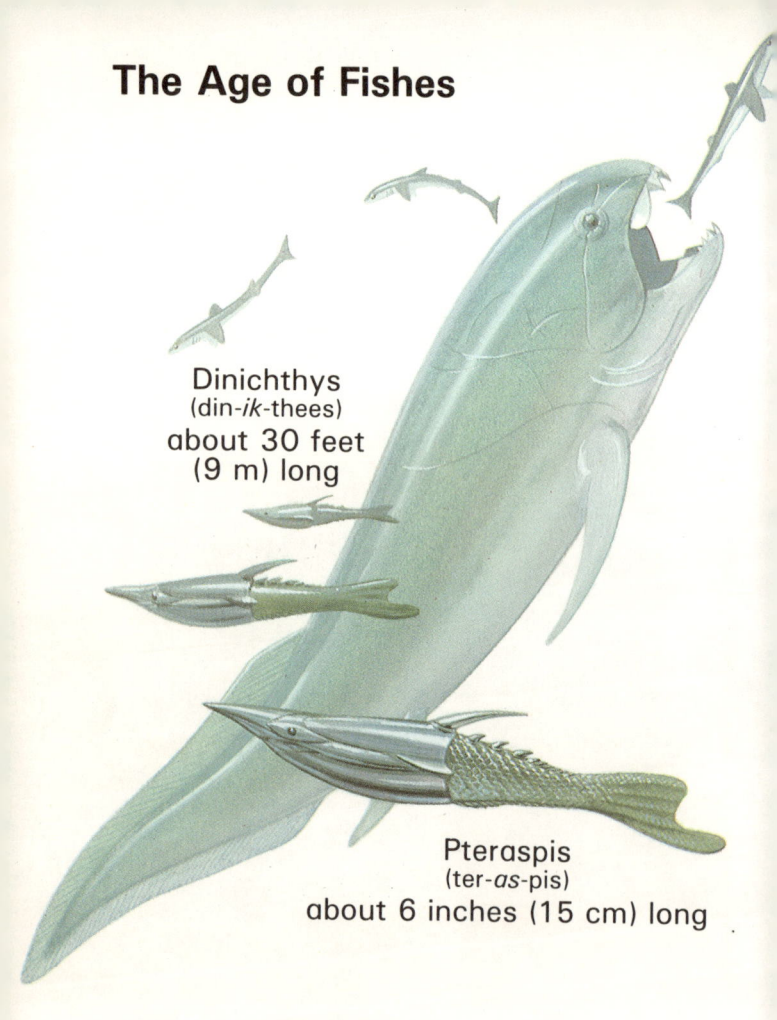

Dinichthys
(din-*ik*-thees)
about 30 feet
(9 m) long

Pteraspis
(ter-*as*-pis)
about 6 inches (15 cm) long

Fish like these
began to live in the sea.
Some were very small.
Some were as long as a bus.

At this time, plants began to grow on the land.
Some were ferns.
There were even tall trees.

Some fish crawled onto the land.

Lobefin fish
1 to 2 feet (30 to 60 cm) long

The world became a drier place.
Many rivers and lakes dried up.
Some fish had very strong fins.
They could crawl onto the land
with these.

The first amphibians (am-*fib*-ee-ans)

Ichthyostega
(ik-thee-o-*stee*-ga)
3 feet (90 cm) long

After millions of years,
some fish grew legs and had lungs.

They had become amphibians.

Amphibians can live on land
and in the water.

A larger amphibian

Eryops
(*air*-re-ops)
5 feet (1.5 m) long

This larger amphibian lived in the warm swamps.

A swamp is a place where water and mud collect.

A very large amphibian

Eogyrinus
(ee-o-*jy*-rin-uss)

Eogyrinus was more than 15 feet (4.5 m) long.

Some amphibians were only 2 inches (5 cm) long.

The first reptiles

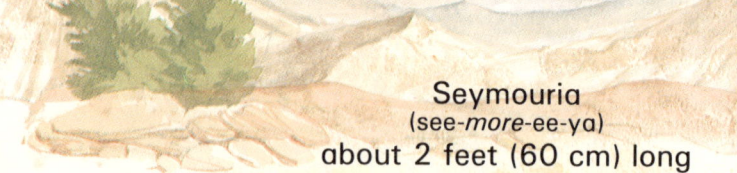

Seymouria
(see-*more*-ee-ya)
about 2 feet (60 cm) long

Slowly, some amphibians changed into reptiles.

This may have been one of the first reptiles.

Edaphosaurus
(ee-daff-o-*sor*-uss)
about 9 feet (2.7 m) long

This fin-backed reptile ate plants.
Reptiles lay their eggs on land.
Amphibians lay their eggs in water.

Another fin-backed reptile

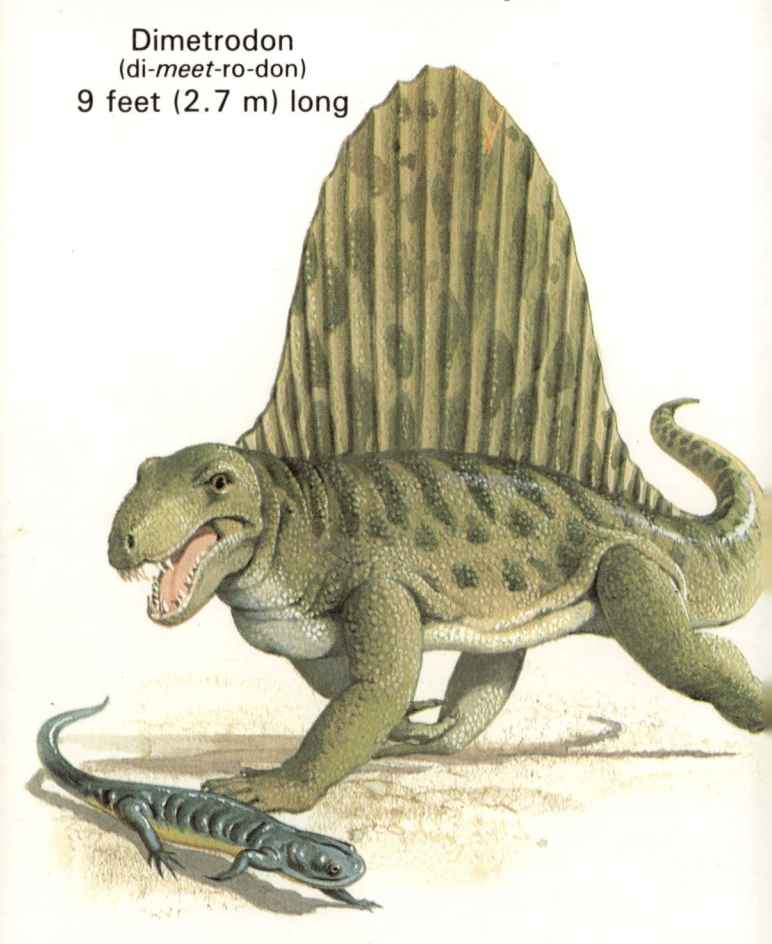

Dimetrodon
(di-*meet*-ro-don)
9 feet (2.7 m) long

Dimetrodon ate meat, not plants.
It probably ate amphibians.

An amphibian and a reptile of today

Frog

Alligator

The frog is an amphibian.
It lays its eggs in the water.
An alligator is a reptile.
It lays its eggs on land.

Sea reptiles

Ichthyosaurus
(ik-thee-o-*sor*-uss)
10 to 40 feet
(3 to 12 m) long

Some reptiles went back to live all the time in the water.

Their eggs were not laid on land.

They hatched inside the females.

Plesiosaurus
(plees-ee-o-*sor*-uss)

Some plesiosaurs were more than 40 feet (12 m) long.

They had very long necks that helped them catch fish.

19

Gliding reptiles

Wing span:
about 1 foot (30 cm)

Pterodactylus
(terr-o-*dak*-till-uss)

Some reptiles grew wings.
The largest had
a wing span of 27 feet (8 m).
Some were no larger than
a small bird.

Wing span: about 4 feet (1.2 m)

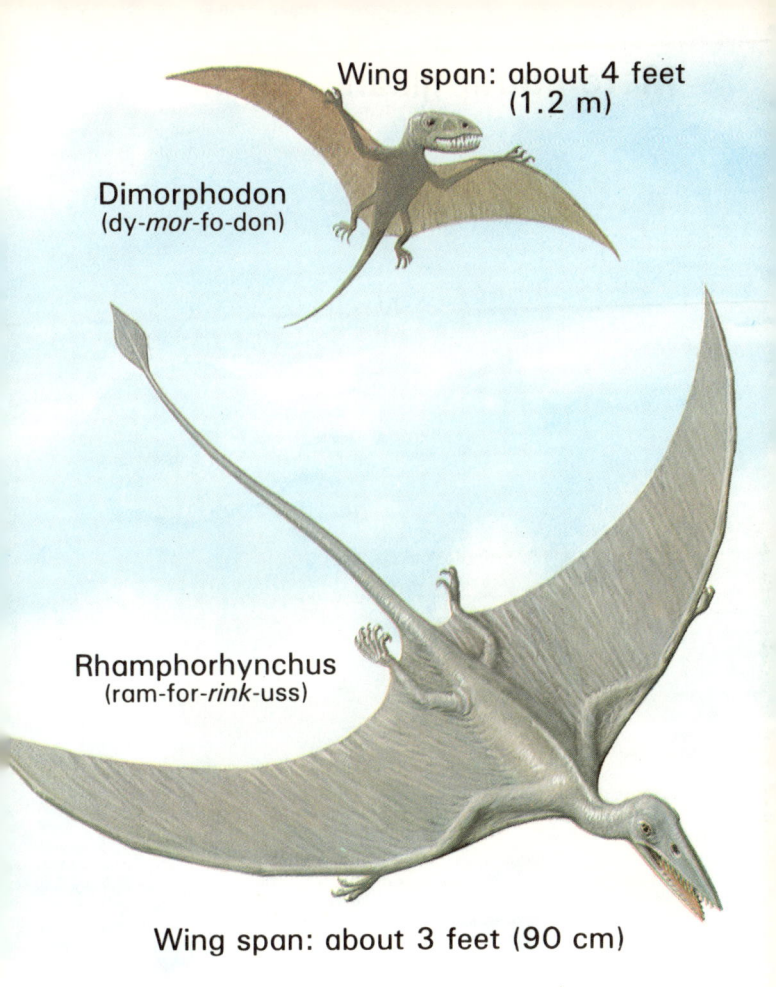

Dimorphodon
(dy-*mor*-fo-don)

Rhamphorhynchus
(ram-for-*rink*-uss)

Wing span: about 3 feet (90 cm)

These reptiles probably glided. They did not fly like birds.

More about gliding reptiles

Gliding reptiles did not have feathers on their wings.

Their wings were made of skin.

They ate fish or small reptiles and insects.

Pteranodon
(ter-*an*-o-don)
**Wing span:
about 25 feet
(8 m)**

Footprints from the past

Huge footprints and very large bones were found in America about 150 years ago.
A skeleton was built with these bones.

A giant skeleton

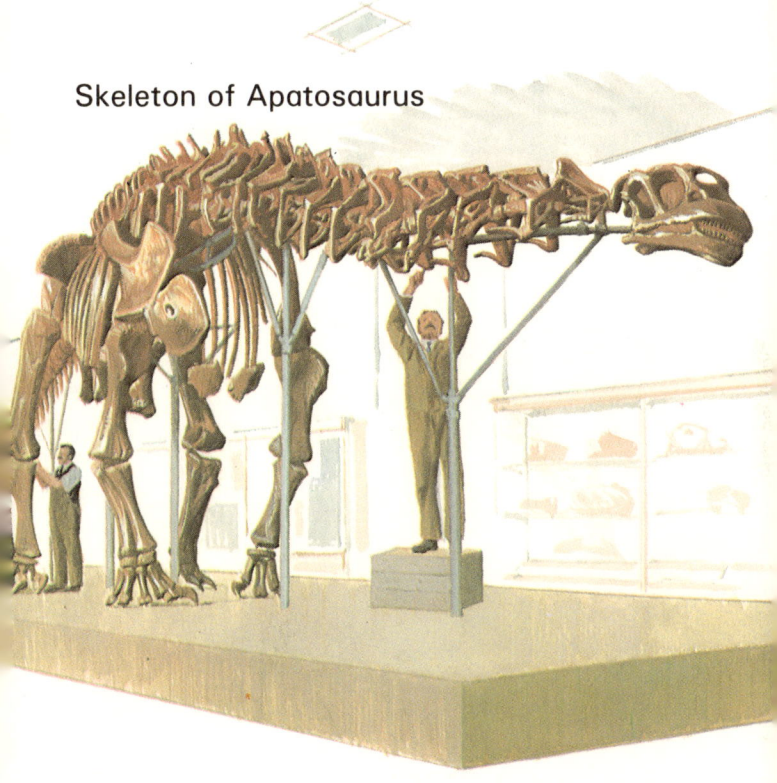

Skeleton of Apatosaurus

The footprints were those of a dinosaur.

So were the bones.

The word "dinosaur" means "terrible lizard."

Diplodocus and Apatosaurus

There were many kinds of dinosaurs.
They lived long before the first men.
Some were very small and quick.
Others were very big and slow.

Apatosaurus
(a-pat-o-*sor*-uss)
65 feet (20 m) long

Diplodocus
(dip-*plod*-o-kuss)
90 feet (27 m) long

The dinosaurs in this picture were very heavy and slow.

They did not like to fight.

They felt safer in the water.

Stegosaurus moved slowly.
It had huge spikes on its tail.
These ripped into attackers.

Stegosaurus
(steg-o-*sor*-uss)
about 20 feet (6 m) long

Antrodemus
(an-tro-*dee*-muss)
about 30 feet (9 m) long

Antrodemus hunted other animals.
Its mouth opened so wide it could swallow small animals whole.
Its back legs were 9 feet (2.7 m) high.

Hypsilophodon and Iguanodon

Hypsilophodon
(hip-sil-*off*-o-don)
up to 6 feet (1.8 m) long

This dinosaur was quite small
and ran very quickly on two legs.

It probably climbed trees
to get away from its enemies.

Iguanodon
(ig-*waan*-o-don)
30 feet (9 m) long

Iguanodon also ate plants, but was larger.

Each front leg had a bony spike.

This spike was used when fighting.

Polacanthus

Polacanthus
(pol-a-*kan*-thuss)
14 feet (4 m) long

The remains of Polacanthus were found in England.

The double row of spikes on its back kept other animals away.

Ankylosaurus

Ankylosaurus
(an-keel-o-*sor*-uss)
15 feet (4.5 m) long

This dinosaur had an almost flat body covered with bony plates.

At the end of its tail was a big lump of bone with spikes.

Ankylosaurus used its tail as a club.

Anatosaurus and Corythosaurus

Anatosaurus
(an-at-o-*sor*-uss)
40 feet (12 m) long

These dinosaurs had webbed fingers and toes.

They lived in swamps and lakes.

Corythosaurus
(cor-ith-o-*sor*-uss)
about 30 feet (9 m) long

Corythosaurus could swim well.
Its name means "helmet reptile."
The bony ridge on its head
looks like a helmet.

Protoceratops

(pro-toe-*sair*-a-tops)
6 feet (2 m) long

In 1922, the fossils of eggs like these were found in Mongolia.

Each egg was about 8 inches (20 cm) long.

Styracosaurus and Tyrannosaurus

Styracosaurus
(sty-rak-o-*sor*-uss)
15 feet (4.5 m) long

This dinosaur looked fierce but ate plants, not other animals.

It had a beak like a parrot's and long spikes on its head.

Triceratops
(try-*sair*-a-tops)
30 feet (9 m) long

Triceratops was a very big and savage fighter.

The two horns above its eyes were more than 3 feet (90 cm) long.

The first real birds

Archaeopteryx
(ar-kee-*op*-terr-iks)

The first real birds lived at the time of the dinosaurs.

They had feathered wings.

These birds were as big as crows.

These birds had teeth like
a reptile's and tails like a lizard's.

The tails were covered with feathers.

The first mammals

Phascolotherium
(fas-kol-o-*theer*-ee-um)

A mammal is an animal that is covered with fur and drinks its mother's milk when it is young.

The first mammals lived at the time of the first birds.

Megatherium
(meg-a-*theer*-ee-um)

The first mammals were
no larger than mice or rats.

Later, some mammals became
much bigger.

This one was 18 feet (5.5 m) high.

More mammals

Uintatherium
(yoo-in-ta-*theer*-ee-um)
about 12 feet (3.5 m) long

This animal was as big as an elephant.

It looked fierce, but did not eat other animals.

Baluchitherium
(bal-oo-kih-*theer*-ee-um)

This animal was three times as tall as a man.

It was about 27 feet (8 m) long and ate leaves and twigs.

The first horses

Eohippus
(ee-o-hip-uss)

Eohippus was the first horse.
It was only 12 inches (30 cm) high.
It had toes, not hooves.

The woolly rhinoceros
8 feet (2.5 m) long

In the Ice Ages, the world became very cold.

The woolly rhinoceros lived then.

Its long, hairy coat kept it warm.

The woolly mammoth

11 feet (3.3 m) high at shoulder

By this time, the first men were living.
They painted pictures of this animal on the walls of their caves.
They killed mammoths for food.

The saber-toothed tiger

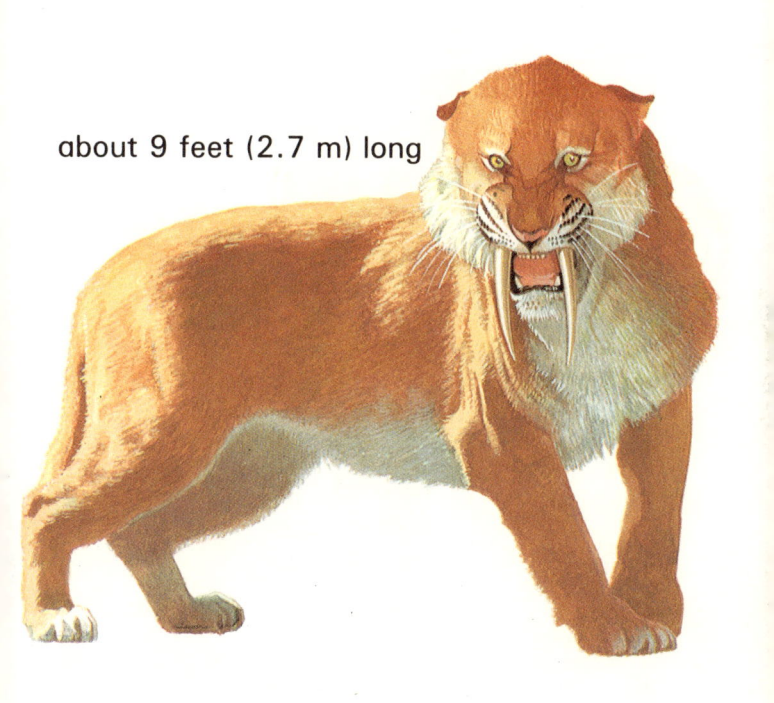

about 9 feet (2.7 m) long

This tiger had front teeth 9 inches (20 cm) long.

It could kill a mammoth or any other animal. But early man hunted the saber-toothed tiger until there were none left.

Index

	page		page
Alligator	17	Fin-backed reptiles	15-16
Ammonite	6	Frog	17
Amphibians	11-17		
Anatosaurus	34	Gliding reptiles	20-23
Ankylosaurus	33		
Antrodemus	29	Horses	48
Apatosaurus	25, 26-27	Hypsilophodon	30
Archaeopteryx	42-43		
		Ice Ages	49
		Ichthyosaurus	18
Baluchitherium	47	Ichthyostega	11
Belemnite	6	Iguanodon	30-31
Birds	42-43		
		Jellyfish	6
Corythosaurus	34-35		
		Lobefin fish	10
Dimetrodon	16		
Dimorphodon	21	Mammals	44-51
Dinichthys	8	Megatherium	45
Dinosaurs	24-41	Monoclonius	40
Diplodocus	26-27		
		Phascolotherium	44
Edaphosaurus	15	Plants	9
Eogyrinus	13	Plesiosaurus	19
Eohippus	48	Polacanthus	32
Eryops	12	Protoceratops	36-37
		Pteranodon	22-23

	page		page
Pteraspis	8	Stegosaurus	28
Pterodactylus	20	Styracosaurus	38
Reptiles	14-41	Swamps	12-13, 34
Rhamphorhynchus	21	Triceratops	40-41
Saber-toothed tiger	51	Trilobite	6
Sea reptiles	18-19	Tyrannosaurus	38-39
Seymouria	14		
Skeleton	24-25	Uintatherium	46
Sponges	6	Woolly mammoth	50
Starfish	6	Woolly rhinoceros	49

Ladybird titles cover a wide range of subjects and reading ages. Write for a free illustrated list from the publishers: **LADYBIRD BOOKS, INC.** Lewiston, Maine 04240